FAT MEN
FROM SPACE

OTHER YEARLING BOOKS YOU WILL ENJOY:

YEARLING BOOKS/YOUNG YEARLINGS/YEARLING CLASSICS are designed especially to entertain and enlighten young people. Patricia Reilly Giff, consultant to this series, received her bachelor's degree from Marymount College. She holds a master's degree in history from St. John's University, and a Professional Diploma in Reading from Hofstra University. She was a teacher and reading consultant for many years, and is the author of numerous books for young readers.

For a complete listing of all Yearling titles,
write to Dell Readers Service,
P.O. Box 1045, South Holland, IL 60473.

FAT MEN
FROM SPACE

Written and illustrated by

DANIEL MANUS PINKWATER

A YEARLING BOOK

Published by
Dell Publishing Co., Inc.
1 Dag Hammarskjold Plaza
New York, New York 10017

Yearling® TM 913705, Dell Publishing Co., Inc.

ISBN: 0-440-44542-6

Reprinted by arrangement with Dodd, Mead & Company

Printed in the United States of America

August 1980

10 9 8

CW

TO S. KILNISAN

(the biggest baby ever born in Budapest)

FAT MEN
FROM SPACE

William went to the dentist. It wasn't so bad—just a filling. The dentist said it wouldn't hurt a bit, and it was almost true. William went home feeling a little bit numb. There was a funny sour taste in his mouth that made him think of electricity. When he sucked in his breath, the tooth with the new filling felt cold. He was able to eat his supper without any trouble, and after watching television with his mother and father, he went to bed.

One of the things William liked to do in bed, and wasn't allowed to, was listen to the radio. William thought that if he had a little radio, with an earphone, he could listen in bed without bothering anybody. He mentioned this to his parents, and found out that not bothering anybody wasn't the point. "I don't want you listening to the radio when you should be sleeping," his mother said. Sometimes William would turn on the radio on the table near his bed, very softly, and try to listen. Usually, his mother would hear it, and tell him to turn it off.

This particular night, after William had been to the

dentist, he was lying in bed listening to the radio. He was listening to a talk show. A man who said he had taken a ride in a flying saucer was telling how the people from outer space were crazy about potato pancakes, and had come to Earth in search of millions of them, which they planned to freeze and take back to their own galaxy. It was a good show, and William was enjoying it. He was ready to drift off to sleep, when he realized that he had never turned the radio on. He checked this. He clicked on the radio next to his bed. It was tuned to a music station. He could still hear the man talking about the flying saucers, over the music. "Are you playing the radio?" his mother shouted from down the hall.

William turned off the radio. The flying-saucer man was still talking. "Can you hear the radio now?" he asked.

"No. Don't turn it on again," his mother said.

His mother could not hear the man talking about the flying saucers. Where was it coming from? William lay very quietly, trying to figure out where the radio program was coming from. It seemed to be coming from inside his head. "Maybe I'm imagining the whole thing," he thought. "Maybe I'm going crazy." It seemed like an ordinary radio program—there wasn't anything crazy about it. He had heard the same talk show before. The announcer was telling people to buy the same bottled spring water, and canned hams, and pianos that always sponsored the program. It was a real radio program going on inside William's head. It worried him. He rubbed the tip of his tongue against the new filling. The volume dropped very low. Wait a second! He did it again. The volume dropped. He pressed his tongue against the tooth. No radio program at all! It was the tooth! The one with the new filling was receiving radio programs! William clenched his teeth. The volume got louder.

"I told you to turn that off!" his mother shouted.

William got up. He went quietly out into the backyard. He clenched his teeth. The radio got louder. He clenched them harder. It got louder still. Keeping his teeth clenched, he pulled his lips back in a big grin. It got so loud that it made an echo. He could hear windows opening, and people shouting, "Turn that thing down!"

" ... *AND THEN THE CAPTAIN OF THE SPACECRAFT ASKED ME IF I KNEW WHERE THERE WERE A LOT OF POTATO PANCAKES,*" the radio tooth said. William jumped up and down. This was wonderful. He didn't know how it worked, but it was wonderful. He had a built-in radio.

William scurried back to bed before anyone could call

9

the cops. He had waked up the whole neighborhood. He was barely able to lie still, he was so excited about his built-in radio. He decided it would be the most fun if he didn't tell anybody about it for a while. Finally, he got tired of planning ways to use his radio tooth, and bored listening to the man talking about flying saucers and potato pancakes. He put his tongue over his tooth and went to sleep.

At breakfast, when William put a spoonful of cornflakes into his mouth, the spoon touched the tooth and changed the station. It had been playing news, but it changed to rock and roll. William took the spoon out—news. He put the spoon back—rock and roll. He tried a fork—news and country and western music at the same time. He put a butter knife into his mouth—classical music.

"William, will you stop playing with the silverware," his father said, "and I think someone left a radio playing upstairs." William put his tongue over his tooth. It wasn't easy to finish breakfast and keep the radio from playing.

At school, William resisted the temptation to use his radio tooth to show off. There were a lot of kids standing around in the schoolyard, waiting for the bell to ring. William stayed by himself, chewing on the wire binding of

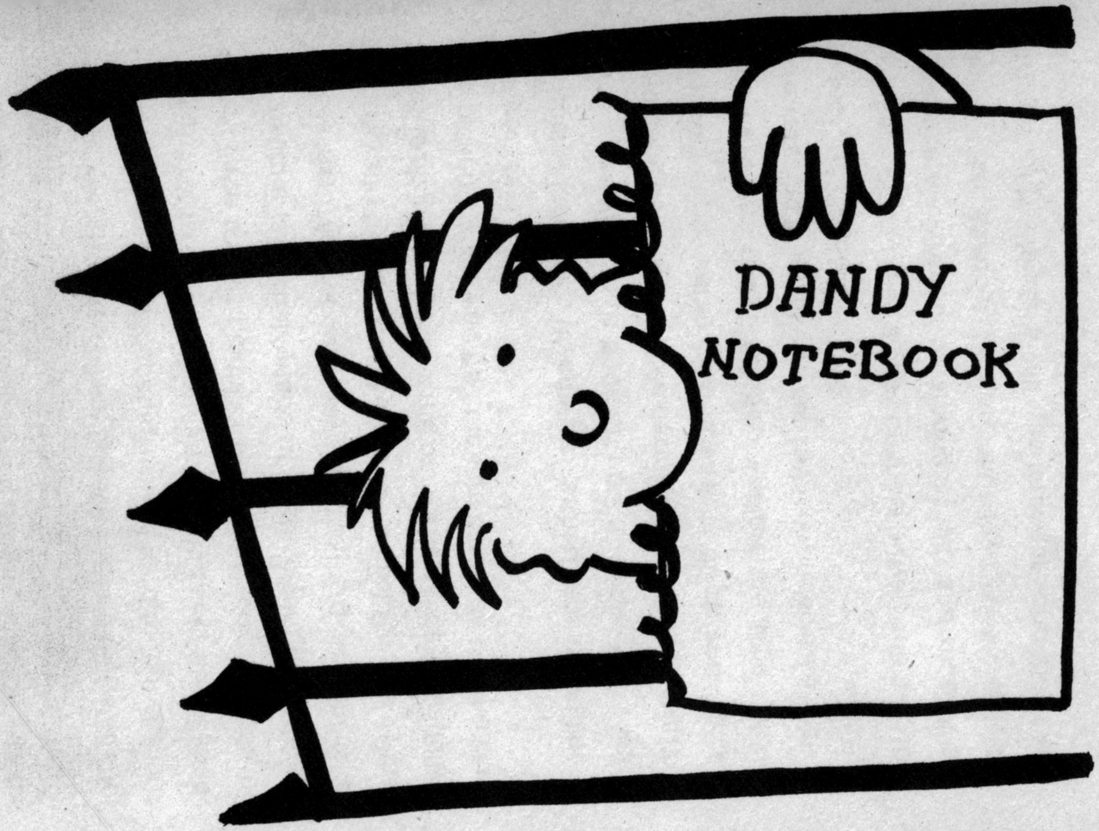
DANDY
NOTEBOOK

his spiral notebook. Depending on where he bit into the wire, he could get different stations.

Mr. Wendel was William's teacher. He didn't stand for any nonsense, and because he was hard to fool, the kids tried to trick him all the time. Nobody ever succeeded. Kids were always planning to put glue on his chair, or substitute fake chalk made of soap. When these things were tried, Mr. Wendel always spotted the glue or the fake chalk, and turned the joke around by asking one of the kids to sit in his chair or write on the blackboard. Usually, he picked the kid who had thought of the trick in the first place.

Lots of kids in Mr. Wendel's class had sent away at one time or another for a book on how to throw your voice. The book came with a little device to hold in your mouth, that was supposed to make it easy to throw your voice. The kids who didn't actually swallow the little voice-throwers had them taken away by Mr. Wendel. It was hard to fool Mr. Wendel.

Other kids had read a book on mind power, and tried to hypnotize Mr. Wendel by staring at him and repeating silently, "Mr. Wendel, you are my slave. . . . My will is stronger." Mr. Wendel's will was stronger—and the kids who had tried to hypnotize him wound up with a new seat near the front of the room, and a note to their parents suggesting an eye examination.

In the classroom, William clenched his teeth. *". . . and then you add the graham crackers to the heated chicken fat. Add paprika, salt, and pepper . . ."* It was a cooking program. All the kids giggled and looked around to see where the noise was coming from. William looked around too. Mr. Wendel didn't say anything. *"Garnish with banana slices in their skin. This festive dish will serve four . . ."* Mr. Wendel walked up and down the aisles, trying to locate the sound. As Mr. Wendel got closer, William unclenched his teeth little by little, so that the sound of the radio got softer. As Mr. Wendel got farther away, he clenched his teeth gradually, so that the sound got louder. He was trying to control the volume so that it seemed to remain constant to Mr. Wendel, wherever he was. Mr. Wendel stopped. William put his tongue over his tooth.

"Melvyn, give me the radio," Mr. Wendel said. He had picked on Melvyn Schwartz—the wrong kid! Nobody knew that he had picked wrong, except William, and Melvyn Schwartz. Mr. Wendel had never picked wrong

13

before. Melvyn was delighted.

"Aw, geez, Mr. Wendel, it isn't fair. You always pick on me," Melvyn said. He was just warming up. "I demand my constitutional rights. You have no reason to accuse me. I demand a trial by a jury of my peers."

"You are peerless, Melvyn," Mr. Wendel said. "Give me the radio."

"I protest," Melvyn said, rising from his desk. "You are persecuting me because of my past misfortunes." Melvyn was the one who had put glue on Mr. Wendel's chair. "I want a lawyer!"

"You will have the best defense that money can buy," Mr. Wendel said. "After that—Devil's Island. Give me the radio."

"I have no radio," Melvyn said, trying to look shifty-eyed and guilty. The class was enjoying this. It was obvious to them that Melvyn was having a lot of fun.

"Melvyn, open your desk," Mr. Wendel said.

"I demand to see your search warrant," Melvyn said.

"Our principal, Mr. Feeney, will be glad to listen to your complaint about illegal search," Mr. Wendel said. "Now, open your desk."

"Storm trooper," Melvyn said, and opened his desk. It was empty, except for Melvyn's history book. "Didn't I tell

14

you?'' Melvyn made a sweeping gesture to the class, which burst into loud applause.

William clenched his teeth, just a little. The radio played faintly.

''Melvyn, empty your pockets,'' Mr. Wendel said. Melvyn emptied his pockets and turned them inside out. No radio. He smiled broadly at Mr. Wendel.

''Melvyn, I apologize for having suspected you,'' Mr. Wendel said.

''I'll never trust anyone in authority again,'' Melvyn said.

William was clenching as hard as he could to get the volume high enough to be heard over the applause and laughter. Melvyn was taking bows from his seat.

''All right, who's got the radio?'' Mr. Wendel asked. A mistake—Mr. Wendel was stumped, and he had shown it. The celebration got louder and louder. ''I'm going to step outside the room for a minute, and when I come back, I want everybody to be quiet and I want the radio to have stopped playing,'' Mr. Wendel said. A miserable trick—it sometimes worked for old lady teachers—the class would think they were crying in the hall, and lay off out of sympathy. It didn't work for Mr. Wendel.

When he came back, an announcer was saying, *"In Chicago a kangaroo is still loose in the streets ... "*

Mr. Wendel was beaten. He fell back on another old tactic. "You are all suspended. You will leave school at once, and not come back until tomorrow *with* a note from your parents."

The idea of a day off from school as a punishment didn't fool anyone. The kids all said "Aww, fooey," and "it isn't fair," as they were expected to, but in their hearts they were thanking the kid with the radio, whoever it was.

A group punishment was easy to explain at home. Every kid's parents would automatically assume that some other kid, and not their little darling, had caused the disturbance.

On the way home with the other kids, William kept his tongue over his tooth and said nothing. Later, he planned to claim credit for the great thing he had done, but for now he was going to enjoy his tooth in secret.

It never occurred to William's mother to ask if William had been one of the kids who misbehaved and got the whole class sent home. She went to the market, leaving William alone with his tooth. He was getting curious about it. Had the dentist put a little radio inside his tooth? Why would he do such a thing?

The dentist was a pretty nice guy. Maybe if William called him up and asked him . . . William looked up the dentist in his mother's little leather telephone book. Dr. Horwitz. He dialed the number. Dr. Horwitz answered. "This is William Pedwee," William said. "Can you tell me something about the tooth you filled for me yesterday?"

"I'll tell you if I can," Dr. Horwitz said.

"What I'd like to know is, why is my tooth receiving radio programs?"

"Your tooth is receiving radio programs? No kidding?" Dr. Horwitz sounded interested.

"Yes, it is," William said. "Did you put a little radio in my tooth?"

"I may have," Dr. Horwitz said, "but it wasn't on purpose. Sometimes when we put a metal filling in a tooth, it reacts with a different kind of metal in another filling. It makes an electric current. It is just possible that a filling could have the properties of a radio receiver, or an old-fashioned crystal set. This isn't a joke, is it, William?"

William told Dr. Horwitz that he was not joking. He gritted his teeth, and Dr. Horwitz heard, *"Tonight at the civic wrestling arena . . . the Human Ape versus Doctor Death! Be sure to see this great match."*

"Was that the tooth?" Dr. Horwitz asked.

"That was it," William said.

"Well, well," Dr. Horwitz said, "I've heard of this happening—once in a million fillings—but it has never happened to me. Tell you what—come right over, and we'll put a coating over that filling, and get rid of those radio programs for you."

"Get rid of them?" William shouted. "Are you kidding? I like my tooth!"

"Oh, you like it, do you?" said Dr. Horwitz. "You just wanted some information. Well, enjoy your tooth, William. If you ever get tired of it, come see me, and we'll fix it up."

William thanked Dr. Horwitz and said good-by.

He was happier than ever about his radio tooth. One in a million, it was. William felt that he was a special person to have such a special tooth.

"And now the number-one tune on the charts, I'll Never Forget Your Nose." William listened to the music as he fished around in his dresser drawer for something to use as an antenna. He found a coil of wire that had come out of an old doorbell he had taken apart. He unwound a few

19

feet of wire and clamped the end between his teeth. *"And that's the local news in the Trinidad, Colorado, area."* William knew he wasn't anywhere *near* Colorado. He listened to the station—sure enough, it was a radio station in Trinidad, Colorado. He let go of the wire, and the station switched back to the familiar local one. *". . . and tonight be sure to tune in when Barry Garble talks to a man who has lived underwater for the past fifteen years."*

William thought of another trick to play with his tooth radio. He had just heard the back door slam. His mother was home from the market. William went downstairs to see her. There was a radio in the kitchen. To turn it on, you pushed a button. To turn it off, you pushed the same button again. William helped his mother put away the groceries. Then he asked her for a cookie and a glass of milk.

While his mother was getting a cookie, William clenched his teeth. *"The President has a cold today, and did not come to work,"* the tooth radio said.

William's mother reached up and pushed the button to turn off the kitchen radio, which turned it on. *"Are you tired? Depressed? Miserable? Stupid? Klunkie's Pills,*

21

made with real extract of chopped chicken livers, will—"

She pushed the button again. William clenched his teeth. *"The President's physician said that the President should get plenty of rest, drink liquids, and stay out of drafts."*

William's mother was getting annoyed. She pushed the button again hard. William unclenched his teeth. The kitchen radio came on. *"Klunkie's Pills cure asthma, chills, fever, and—"*

She pushed the button so hard that the radio almost fell off the shelf. William clenched his teeth. *"Back in 1957, President Eisenhower had a cold—"*

She pushed the button. She was getting red in the face. *". . . malaria, mange, baldness, pimples, thrips—"*

William's mother pulled the plug. "What is wrong with this radio?" she said. "I'll have your father look at it when he gets home."

William was almost choking on the cookie. He was having a hard time not laughing. Before he left the room, he clenched his teeth for a couple of seconds. *"President Coolidge had a cold in . . ."* William's mother looked at the dangling plug. William had to run upstairs so she wouldn't hear him laughing.

When William's father came home, he spent a lot of time whispering in the kitchen with William's mother. That wasn't usual, but William didn't pay any special attention to it. At the supper table he noticed that his parents were smiling and winking at each other quite a lot. He thought they must be in an extra good mood.

"Something is wrong with the kitchen radio," William's mother said. William waited, and listened to the radio station inside his head. A station break was coming. He clenched. *This is WXXO Radio—*

"Did someone say radio?" William's father asked.

William clenched. *". . . radio all day and all night—"*

"Have some carrots," William's mother said.

William clenched his teeth as hard as he could. *"AND NOW THE NEWS. TODAY A LARGE CARDBOARD CARTON OF FROZEN POTATO PANCAKES WAS SIGHTED FLOATING IN OUTER SPACE—"*

"Do you want some more milk, William?" his mother said.

What was wrong? Why couldn't his parents hear the radio? William had been clenching his teeth as hard as he could. The radio tooth was so loud it almost gave him a headache.

23

"You'll never guess who I met downtown today," William's father said. "It was Dr. Horwitz, the dentist who takes care of William's teeth."

"He's an awfully nice man," William's mother said. She was starting to giggle.

"Yes he is," William's father said, "a very nice man, and so interesting. He told me some fascinating things about dentistry."

So that was it. Horwitz had finked. William decided that he was going to bite Dr. Horwitz's finger one of these days.

"And guess who happened to come by while we were talking," William's father went on.

"Who was it, dear?" William's mother was laughing so hard she could hardly talk.

"It was Mr. Wendel, William's teacher," his father said, "and *he* had something fascinating to tell us. It seems that someone in William's class was playing a radio today, and Mr. Wendel just couldn't find it. The poor man finally had to send the whole class home."

"That certainly is fascinating," William's mother said. She was laughing so hard now that she had to hang onto the table to keep from falling out of her chair. "And what did Dr. Horwitz have to say about dentistry that was so fascinating?''

''It seems that Dr. Horwitz had just done a filling for one of his patients, and that filling turned out to work just like a radio.''

''Imagine that,'' William's mother said. ''Was the patient anyone we know?''

''Now, let me think,'' his father said. ''I believe it was someone we know. Now who was it? Oh, yes! It was our very own son, William!''

William's father and mother were both helpless with laughter. He hated it when they got this way. He was good and mad. Why did Dr. Horwitz have to go blabbing things? And why did Mr. Wendel have to turn up, and make things worse? Some day he was going to get even with those guys.

William's parents were finished laughing, and were now at the wet-eyed and sighing stage. William got ready for the serious part.

''William, Mr. Wendel understands that there will be no more problems with radios in school,'' his father said, ''and Dr. Horwitz is of the opinion that your tooth will settle down in a day or two and stop receiving—but if it doesn't, he can see you on Saturday and put a nice coating of epoxy on it. Meanwhile, no more tricks, and no listening to your tooth in bed. Now, see if you can get me the baseball scores on your molar, son.'' At this point, William's father collapsed into laughter again. William got up and walked straight out of the kitchen, into the backyard. He was disgusted. Adults never know a good thing when they see it. His tooth was one in a million, and his parents thought it was a big joke.

William stood in the backyard. He could hear his parents laughing inside the house. They thought the whole thing was funny. They didn't care that they had just ruined everything for their only son. William was angry and miserable. It wasn't going to be very much fun, having a one-in-a-million tooth, if it was going to be coated with epoxy in a few days. "If I ever have a little boy, and he is lucky enough to get a radio tooth, I'm going to do everything I can to help him enjoy it,'' William thought.

William fished the piece of wire, the part of a taken-apart doorbell, out of his pocket. He played with the wire, idly, while standing in the backyard. It was a heavy, damp night. There was a storm brewing somewhere. Already, William could see a little glow in the sky now and then—lightning a long way off. He put one end of the wire in his

26

mouth. *"In East Trinidad, there will be a meeting of the Cowboy's Mah Jong Club, behind the feed store at seven-thirty."* It was that station in Trinidad, Colorado. It was coming in very clear. William remembered that he had planned to try out a longer piece of wire. He had some up in his room, but he didn't want to go back into the house. He didn't want to see his mother and father. He was still mad at them. Then William had a bright idea.

All around the backyard was a metal chain-link fence. William could wrap one end of his piece of wire around a fence post, and the whole thing would act as one immense antenna. He cheered up. "I bet I get to hear China," he said.

William twisted one end of his wire around a fence post. The other end he put in his mouth. Then he had a very unusual experience. He felt a thumping—like the thumping of a bass drum—and he heard a sort of rushing, buzzing noise. And he saw amazing colors, purple and red and blue. And his body did things all by itself. All these things seemed to be going on for a long time, but William knew they were happening very fast. And while all those things were happening, William was remembering all he knew about static electricity. He thought about when it is cold and dry, and you rub your feet on the carpet—and

27

you touch the doorknob, and there is a snap, and you can see a little spark. It seemed to William that the chain-link fence had stored up a very big charge of static electricity, and William had bitten right into it. He noticed that he was lying in the grass and having a hard time catching his breath. Nothing hurt him, but he had a very funny taste in his mouth.

Then William noticed that his tooth was not receiving. At first, he thought the tooth had gone completely dead. Then he was able to hear some faint static. But there was no program. There was no WXXO. William clenched his teeth. The static got louder. William listened. He was lying in the grass, where he had landed when he got the shock. The static was kind of rhythmical, like music. It was interesting. William thought it was almost like a language.

The more William listened to the strange static, the more he felt that he could almost understand it. It wasn't as though he could hear words coming through the crackling and whistling. It was the noise itself that had meaning. When William tried to listen hard, it was difficult to understand. When he just relaxed, and half-paid attention, it was almost possible to understand.

"William, we're going now. We'll be visiting across the

street. Don't lie there in the grass all evening." It was William's parents. A few months ago, there had been some big arguments about baby-sitters. William had finally persuaded his parents that he was old enough to be left by himself, at least when they were not going any farther away than the house of a neighbor across the street.

"I'll go in soon," William said. "I'm just looking at the sky." He was not exactly lying. He was looking at the sky, while listening to the strange rhythmic static on his tooth. It looked as though it might not rain after all. The clouds were breaking up, and a few stars were showing.

The static was starting to make sense. It wasn't like anything William had ever heard. He knew what the noises meant. He could tell the directions they came from. The noises were spacemen talking to one another.

Somehow, William's tooth had been converted to receive the signals between the spacemen. Probably the charge of static electricity had done it. The static told William more than words ever did. He could tell that there were a number of different spacemen talking. Some were far away in spaceships, some were on the Earth. William could tell where the spacemen were in relation to one another. He could tell how fast they were moving, and in which direction. It was almost as if he could see the spaceships. It was like listening to a baseball game on the radio. He could see the players in their various positions. As new information came over the radio, William could move the players in his mind—play the game in his mind.

This was better than a baseball game. The field was thousands of miles—millions of miles. The players were spaceships that moved with such speed, they could go so fast and so far, that they would disappear in seconds and reappear in some other part of the sky. They reminded William of those bugs that scoot on the surface of water in summer.

William was listening to twenty or thirty conversations at once. He had no trouble sorting them out. He could tell where each spaceman was, and what he was talking about. Some of the conversations were about potato pancakes. Some spacemen were assembling huge piles of potato pancakes in remote places on Earth. Spaceships would come and collect the potato pancakes and speed away with them. Other conversations were about navigation, and spaceships keeping in touch with one another. Some of the conversations were about a boy, an earth-boy who was listening in. The spacemen knew that William was listening! It made him shiver.

One of the spaceships was getting closer! As it got closer, the static from the spaceship got louder and clearer. It seemed to William that the spaceship was getting bigger and bigger. It was zooming toward him. William decided to get up and go inside the house. He discovered that he couldn't move. He couldn't even twitch a finger. He could see the spaceship—a spot of light, a long way off. It was getting bigger and bigger. He could see it clearly. It was saucer-shaped, and glowing and spinning. The static from the spaceship was so loud that William couldn't even hear his heart, which was pounding. Now the spaceship was directly over him, and falling. He was sure the thing was going to crush him. The static kept telling him not to be scared, but he was scared anyway. He was good and scared.

The saucer stopped falling, and just hung in the air, about twenty feet above him. William could see that it was made of metal. It had a reddish color, that changed to blue or green from time to time. It was spinning slowly, and rocking slightly from side to side. Up till now, William had not thought of screaming for help. He thought of it

now, and gave it a try. The static was so loud that he couldn't tell if anything was getting out.

He was still screaming, or trying to, when he started floating up. He was moving through the air slowly, as though something were drawing him up toward the spaceship, and he was spinning with the spaceship. It was a weird feeling. William didn't like it. It must have taken about a minute for William to spin and float up to the saucer. When he had almost reached it, a hole appeared in the metal skin of the thing. It wasn't like a door; it was a round hole that appeared in the metal, very small, and got larger as William got closer. As he passed through it, the hole closed again under him. He knew this because he found himself lying on a solid metal floor the moment he had gone through.

All around him were cardboard cartons. They were ordinary cartons, the kind that pile up behind the supermarket. They had advertising for cigarettes and toilet tissues printed on them. They were all different sizes and shapes, and they were all full of potato pancakes, fresh and frozen.

William discovered he could move again. He had a look at the room he was in. It was glowing with a greenish light that seemed to come from everywhere. The walls and floor and ceiling were made of metal. There was a little round thing on the ceiling, made of shiny metal. It was about the size of a tennis ball, and covered with little bumps. The room seemed to be a sort of storage room or closet.

"You have been captured by a spaceburger from the planet Spiegel." It was the little round thing talking—a sort of loudspeaker. It was making the same sort of static noise that William had been receiving on his tooth. He understood it perfectly. "No harm will come to you. You will be treated fairly, and returned to your home," the speaker went on. William was good and scared, even though the little round metal thing had told him that no harm would come to him.

"I want to go home," William said.

"That is not possible at this time," the speaker said, "but we will let you out of the storage hold."

"Fine," William said, "let me out."

"First you must promise that you will not attempt to harm the spaceburger, and that you will abide by the regulations governing spacemen on board this craft."

"I promise," William said.

"Also you must promise not to tell anyone about the things you see and hear on the spaceburger," the speaker said.

"I won't say a word," William said.

"In a few seconds a door will open, and you may go up the ladder," the speaker said.

William was a little scared at the thought of meeting the spacemen. He had seen a lot of science-fiction movies. Maybe they were green and scaly, like lizards. Maybe they had heads like flies, with big weird fly-eyes. Maybe they were like green weeds, and talked in horrible whispers.

There was nothing to do but go and find out. A door opened—it just appeared in the wall, like the round hole William had floated through when he had been brought on board, and beyond it a ladder. William climbed the ladder. The ladder took him up into a metal corridor. It was glowing green like the storage hold, only brighter. It was hot in the corridor, and William could hear something buzzing. He had an idea that he was somewhere near the engine, or whatever made the spaceburger go.

William walked along the corridor until he came to the end. There weren't any doors, just smooth metal walls, glowing green. At the end of the corridor was another
36

round shiny metal speaker, like the one in the storage hold. "Are you out there?" the speaker said.

"Yes," William said. A door appeared, and William stepped into a room. He could tell it was the control room of the spaceburger. It looked like the control room of all the spaceships he had seen in movies, and on TV. There were lots of TV screens and flashing lights, and panels of buttons and dials. There was also a deep-fryer and a soft ice cream machine.

The spacemen weren't at all what William had expected. They looked like ordinary earth-people, except that they were fatter than most. William guessed that they weighed at least 350 pounds apiece. There were seven or eight of them. They didn't have the sort of uniforms that William had always seen spacemen wearing in movies. All the spacemen were wearing plaid sport jackets, and dacron slacks. They had knitted neckties, and black-and-white shoes with thick rubber soles. They all had crew cuts and they all wore eyeglasses made of heavy black plastic. The only thing about their clothing that was sort of nifty and spacemanlike was their belts. The belts were wide and made out of white plastic. They had silver buckles in the shape of a cheeseburger with a bolt of

37

lightning going through it. Some of the spacemen had tie clips with the same design.

"I am Hanam, the Captain of this spaceburger," one of the spacemen said. "We apologize for having to capture you, but we had a bad experience not long ago. It seems one of our spaceburgers picked up an earth person, and, even though he promised not to say anything about it, as soon as he was released, he went on a radio program and blabbed about everything he had seen. We can't take the chance that you'll do the same thing—especially now, so close to the invasion."

"Invasion?" William said. "Are you going to invade Earth?"

"Of course we are," Hanam said. "Don't you ever go to the movies? Spacemen always invade places. We have been collecting all the potato pancakes we can find and shipping them back to our leader, Sargon, on the planet Spiegel—they're his favorite. Now that we have collected most of the potato pancakes, we are getting ready to invade."

"But why do you want to invade Earth?" William asked. "We never did anything to hurt you."

"Because we are pirates," Hanam said, "space pirates.

38

All we do is invade planets and take whatever we want. Then we go back to Spiegel, and have big celebrations. After a while, we go out and invade some more planets. It's a lot of fun."

"There aren't very many of you," William said.

"Oh, there are very many of us, all right." Hanam said. "This is just a potato-pancake collecting ship. The main fleet will be arriving any time now. Then the fun begins."

William was very worried by the things Hanam was saying. He was afraid the spacemen would hurt his mother and father. He had seen movies in which spacemen came to Earth with death rays and things that shot fire and turned people to mush. "Do you have death rays?" William asked, "Are you going to knock down all the tall buildings in Tokyo and Los Angeles?"

"Mercy, no," Hanam said. "We don't do anything nasty like that. All we do when we invade a planet is walk around and have a snack, and we don't pay for it either. After a while we use up all the things we came to get, and then we enslave the local population, and get them to produce more of the things we like. That's all. We don't do anything destructive."

Hanam seemed very friendly, but William still didn't like

the idea of Earth being invaded. "In other words you come to steal things," William said.

"Plunder," Hanam said, "plunder's the word. It's traditional."

"Are you going to let me go home?" William asked.

"After we get started plundering, we'll put you down near the place we picked you up," Hanam said. "Meanwhile, just keep out of the way and enjoy your ride. Now I have to get back to work. You may look out the porthole if you like."

William was standing near a round window in the side of the spaceburger. He walked over and looked out. What he saw was amazing. He could see the whole Earth—or most of it. The spaceburger had gotten very high since he had been taken on board. He could see North America, and parts of South America and Europe. It was like the globe in Mr. Wendel's classroom, only the colors were much nicer. Everything was sort of shimmering and glowing, and reflecting the light of the moon. There were clouds like strings of yarn near the earth, and the oceans and big lakes shimmered beautifully. William really liked it. That is, he really liked the Earth—not just the sight he was enjoying. He felt that the Earth was a wonderful place. It was his home and he liked it. It made him feel sort of strange and sad. It made him feel sadder to think that the Earth was going to be invaded, and the people enslaved by these fat spacemen. William wondered what he could do about it—but he was just a kid. There was nothing he could do.

His radio tooth was starting to work again. He had been too busy to pay attention to it, but he had been vaguely aware of the fact that it hadn't been receiving since he came on board the spaceburger. Now, standing near the glass or plastic window, it was starting to pick up faint signals again. William thought that maybe the metal spaceburger stopped the radio waves, but they could pass through the stuff the porthole was made of.

The signals were not as loud and clear as they had been on Earth, but if William clenched his teeth hard, he could make them out. There was the static-language of the spacemen communicating. Moving through space, William wasn't able to make a mental picture of the movements of the spaceships as easily as before. He did get the impression of a lot of activity. There seemed to be more and more of the spaceburgers every minute. William strained to try and see them. Every now and then, he did see a brief flash of reflected light that might have been another spaceburger.

William could also hear the radio station on Earth that had always come through on his tooth. It was very faint, and he had to clench his teeth so hard to hear it that it gave him a headache. He could only keep it up for a few seconds at a time. The radio station was broadcasting news flashes, and they were very interesting.

"Flash—the millions of round objects falling slowly through space are not meteorites as previously thought, but have now been identified as fat men, wearing plaid sport jackets, falling slowly into our atmosphere. Stay tuned to this station for further reports on the amazing story."

The invasion had started. William hoped his mother and father weren't too scared.

"Reports from our affiliated stations seem to indicate that the fat men have started to land. It is estimated that there are hundreds of millions of them still in the sky. The fat men are landing in all parts of the world, but the greatest concentrations appear to be in California and New Jersey."

William looked around. All the fat men, except Hanam,

43

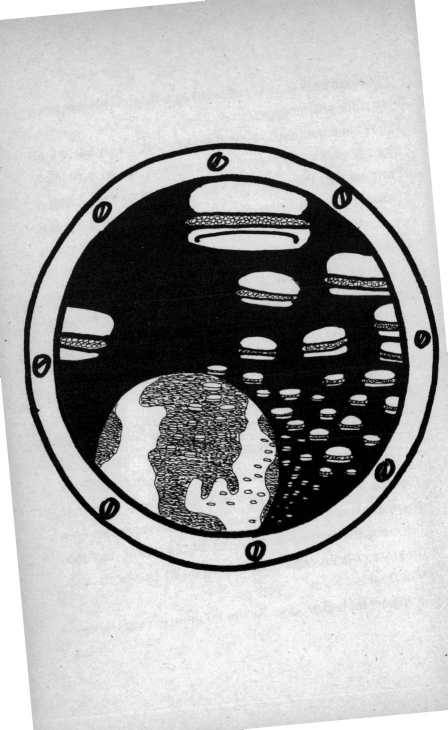

were buttoning their plaid sport jackets, and putting their black plastic-rimmed eyeglasses in their pockets—preparing to jump. Hanam was standing at the controls, operating the spaceburger. A door appeared in the side of the spaceburger, and the crew jumped out. William looked out the porthole and saw the fat men slowly tumbling their way toward Earth.

"There is widespread panic all over Earth, as the hordes of fat men from space continue to land. So far there have been no reports of hostile acts. The governments of all the countries of Earth have asked people to remain calm, and stay in their houses until the invaders express their intentions. We will keep you informed as this amazing story develops."

William could see lots of other spaceburgers now. He saw hundreds of fat spacemen tumble by his porthole. There were spaceburgers dropping spacemen as far as William could see. The only clear places were over the oceans. Everywhere else, there were spacecraft and jumpers. It really was an amazing sight. William couldn't remember ever seeing so many of anything.

"What do these fat men from space want? Is this the beginning of a war? Do they want to conquer the people

45

of Earth?. . . It appears that, for the moment, they want hamburgers. . . . Crowds of fat men have surrounded roadside hamburger stands throughout the civilized world. . . . They are also consuming great quantities of pizza, and cupcakes wrapped in cellophane . . . and hot dogs . . . and ice cream bars . . . and jelly doughnuts . . . halvah . . . chocolate-covered marshmallows. . . . It seems that the invaders from space are after every sort of junk food. . . . Stand by for further bulletins.''

William was starting to get the picture now. He was beginning to understand what sort of pirates these were. The news bulletins were coming faster and faster now.

''No cars, trains, or buses are able to move because of gangs of fat men from space strolling on the roads, eating Twinkies and jumbo cheeseburgers. Airplanes all over the world are grounded by the fat men who are continuing to fall earthward . . .''

''It is next to impossible to make one's way through any of the great cities of Earth because of the clutter of popsicle sticks and empty paper cups in the street . . .''

''Conditions of panic exist in many parts of the United States. Residents of most areas cannot get anything to eat but lean meat, fish, fruit, and vegetables . . .''

46

"A late-breaking bulletin from San Anselmo, California—fat men from space broke into a warehouse and ate sixty thousand frozen tacos . . ."

"On State Highway 22 in New Jersey, fat men from space held two sixteen-year-old girls captive for six hours at Burger World, until the girls had finished deep-frying 148,000 orders of breaded clams . . ."

"The Pentagon announced, a few minutes ago, that there is no more whipped cream left anywhere on Earth. General Fred Horsewhistle, speaking for the Joint Chiefs of Staff, expressed the opinion that it may be necessary to use nuclear weapons against the fat men, whatever the cost. Stand by for further bulletins."

William could see that the situation was very serious. The fat men from space were eating up all the junk food on Earth at a fantastic rate. What worried him was what Hanam had told him about enslaving the people of Earth to make more junk food for them, after they had eaten everything on Earth. He was alone in the spaceburger with Hanam, who was operating the controls, and munching on a frozen pizza. William wondered if he could overpower Hanam in some way, and get to Earth to warn everybody about what was going to happen next. He

47

decided there was no way. He didn't know how to operate the spaceburger, and besides Hanam was much bigger than he was. William just looked out of the porthole, and listened to his tooth.

"In Cleveland, Ohio, spacemen are preparing to dynamite the locked doors of the White Palace frozen hamburger vault, containing one-fourth of the hamburgers on Earth. Mankind will never recover from this massive onslaught against its hamburger reserves."

The hours passed, and the news flashes continued. William had taken a nap, and Hanam had let him make himself a milkshake and a frozen Mexican dinner. When William looked out the porthole, the fat men were still continuing to fall through the sky.

"In Coney Island, New York, hot dog men made a brave attempt to defend Nathan's famous hot dog stand against a large gang of fat spacemen. After a fierce battle, lasting several hours, the hot dog men were overpowered, and tied up with strings of their own hot dogs, forced to watch while the fat men devoured all the steamed corn, and French-fried potatoes. This is one of the most heartbreaking and tragic stories of the current emergency, and citizens of Brooklyn have already stated their inten-

tion to erect a monument to the brave hot dog men when normal conditions return . . ."

"A news flash—the White House has been invaded by the spacemen who have carried off the President's private store of frozen Milky Way bars. As soon as Congress can make its way through the welter of empty fish-and-chips boxes that are obstructing traffic in the Capitol, it is expected that war will be declared against wherever the fat men come from."

William thought this was getting serious. "You spacemen had better leave, before war is declared," he said to Hanam.

"That doesn't worry us," Hanam said. "You don't have any weapons that we can't eat."

It looked extremely bad for Earth. William had just heard that the fat men had found the Holloway's Milk Duds factory in Chicago, and cleaned it out. Giant chocolate factories in Hershey, Pennsylvania, were deserted. Not a crumb or a person was left. Whole populations were making their way out of cities, stumbling on foot through the piles of wastepaper, cartons, and wrappers. Families tried to escape into the hills or the country, carrying a bag of marshmallows, or a Three Musketeers bar. In almost

49

every case, squads of fat men intercepted the fugitives, and took away their last bit of junk food.

William knew that when the spacemen had gobbled all the cheeseburgers and pizzas and doughnuts, they would enslave the people of Earth and make them produce more things for the invaders to eat. It looked hopeless. It looked dismal. He looked at Hanam. Hanam was licking his fingers. He had just finished an ice-cream pop and a bottle of birch beer. He was idly working the levers and buttons that controlled the spaceburger. An orange light was flashing on the instrument panel, and a high-pitched beeper was beeping. It seemed to be a signal of some sort. Hanam shot a nervous look at William, and went back to minding the controls.

William looked out the porthole. There was a tremendous stirring in the space above Earth. It looked to William as though the fat men were falling upward. They were falling upward! They were tumbling up from Earth, just the way they had tumbled down. William looked at Hanam. Hanam looked worried and preoccupied. "What's happening?" William asked. Hanam didn't answer.

William tried to tune in on the static-language. There

was so much talking going on that William had a hard time making out what was being said. Something about a potato pancake—the usual topic. Why all this activity, and excitement? William clenched and tuned in the radio station. *"More reports are coming in every minute to the effect that the spacemen appear to be leaving Earth. This radio station will keep you informed of this surprising development."*

There was a thumping on the outside of the space-burger. A door appeared and first one, then another of the crew tumbled in. They seemed excited. Another thumping, and more spacemen came aboard. "What's going on?" William asked.

"We're leaving," Hanam said. "As soon as the rest of the crew come aboard, we'll be off for another solar system. You see, a message just came through from Sargon. There is a report of a giant potato pancake launched in space in the vicinity of the planet Ziegler. We're going to go after it. It sounds like the biggest potato pancake ever sighted."

"What about me?" William asked. "You said you were going to take me home."

"There won't be time for that," Hanam said. "A potato

pancake like this, a wild one floating in space, turns up once in fifty years. You'll have to come along."

"But when will you take me home?" William asked.

"We might come this way in six or seven hundred years," Hanam answered. "We'll drop you off then."

"Six or seven hundred years!" William said. "I'll be an old man by then! I want to go home now!"

"I don't see how we can do that," Hanam said. "We have to leave as soon as the last two crew members come aboard."

"You promised to take me home!" William shouted. "I don't want to go with you. I don't want to go chasing a wild potato pancake in outer space for seven hundred years! I want to go home right now!"

"Well, the only thing I can suggest is that you float down," Hanam said.

"I don't know how to float down," William said.

"There's nothing to it, if you have a spacejacket," Hanam said. "We can give you a spare, and drop you right away."

Hanam reached into a locker and pulled out a plaid sport jacket. "Here, try this on," he said.

William tried the jacket on. It was about fifty sizes too

large. It came right down to his feet.

"All you have to do is jump," Hanam said. A door appeared.

"I'm not sure I understand," William said. Hanam pushed him out the door.

Once he got used to it, William liked falling through space. The only thing that bothered him was that he couldn't tell if he was falling fast or slow. As he tumbled down, droves of fat spacemen passed him, falling in the other direction—falling upward. It took William quite a while to fall through space, and while he was falling he thought things over. If he understood it correctly, the plaid sport jacket was supposed to break his fall in some way. He hoped that was the way it worked. Otherwise, he was going to make a little hole in the ground when he hit.

William looked at the map of North America below him. He wondered if he would land anywhere near home. Gradually the map turned into a model railroad landscape of mountains and trees, towns and lakes. He knew he was falling slowly, like a snowflake, now. He felt like a snowflake—it was cold, high up in the atmosphere. William passed through clouds, slowly. The clouds were wet and unpleasant, not at all the way William thought they would

feel. He pulled the plaid spacejacket tight around him.

As William got closer to Earth, he could see individual houses and cars. Now and then a few spacemen would float up past him. William guessed that most of them had already returned to their spaceburgers. William realized that his float-down was almost over, and he felt a little sad. It had been the best part of the whole experience.

William floated down, and landed on the sidewalk in front of his house! He gave a little push with his feet, and floated over the house into the backyard. He did one more experimental jump, straight up, of about a hundred feet, landed lightly, took off the spacejacket, folded it neatly, and went into the house.

Everything was normal inside the house, except that the door had been ripped off the freezer. William's mother told him later that some fat men had broken in and taken all the TV dinners, the sugar-coated breakfast cereal, and the instant breakfast powder.

William's parents were glad to see him. They had been worried about him, of course, but during the emergency it had been impossible to get in touch with the police. William's father had tried to go out and look for him, but he never got past the enormous piles of Big Mac boxes in the road. So William's mother and father just sat at home during most of the invasion from outer space, eating the shredded wheat and lettuce that the spacemen had left them, and hoping their son was all right.

William put the spacejacket carefully away in his closet. He didn't have much time to enjoy it. School and most kinds of work had been suspended for several weeks, and the people on Earth devoted themselves to a massive effort to clean-up the litter. William and his parents were out every day with rakes and shovels, and came home tired every night to their green salad and whole-grain bread, milk, and sometimes meat. William and his parents got to enjoy the clean-up work, and even the experience of living without cheeseburgers and pizza. After the clean-up was finished, the government announced it would be at least a year before soda pop, taco chips, and a lot of other things were once again in general supply. There was almost no sugar anywhere on Earth, which turned out to be much less of a hardship than people expected.

William's parents seemed to have forgotten about the radio tooth. William didn't see any point in mentioning it to them. It still worked, although not as well as it had before the shock from the metal fence, and the adventure in the spaceburger. Sometimes the tooth would be silent for days at a time, and sometimes it would play fairly well. When William went to the dentist a year later, the tooth hadn't played for almost a month, and Dr. Horwitz thought it would probably stop playing altogether after a while. He also told William that he had no new cavities—a common occurrence worldwide, since sugar was still scarce.

But the radio tooth was not entirely dead. Some nights it would play quite well, and on special nights—ones that were clear and cold—William could hear, behind the Barry Garble show, a kind of rhythmic static that was almost like a language.